Emmy
the Exaggerating
Elephant

Fenton
the Fearful Frog

Gertie
the Grungy Goat

Herbie
the Happy
Hamster

Ivy
the Impatient
Iguana

Ollie
the Obedient
Ostrich

Perry
the Polite
Porcupine

Queenie
the Quiet Quail

Rupert
the Resourceful
Rhinoceros

Wendy
the Wise
Woodchuck

Xavier
the X-ploring
Xenops

Yori
the Yucky Yak

Ziggy
the Zippy Zebra

W9-DID-217

NOTE TO PARENTS

Take One Home Free
A story about subtracting

In this story, Emmy the Exaggerating Elephant bakes ten pies and sets them out on a table to cool. As each of ten AlphaPets takes one pie away, your child will see how the quantity of pies diminishes, one by one, until the pies are all gone.

In addition to enjoying this story with your child, you can use it to help your child grasp the concept of subtraction and understand the relationship between a numeral and the quantity it stands for.

When you've finished reading the story together, your child will enjoy doing the activity at the end of the book.

The AlphaPets™ characters were conceived and created by Ruth Lerner Perle.
Characters interpreted and designed by Deborah Colvin Borgo.
Cover/book design and production by Norton & Company.
Logo design by Deborah Colvin Borgo and Nancy S. Norton.
Printed and Manufactured in the United States of America

Take One Home Free

RUTH LERNER PERLE

Illustrated by Richard Max Kolding

Grolier Enterprises Inc., Danbury, Connecticut

One day, Emmy the Exaggerating Elephant went to the AlphaPet supermarket. After she took a shopping cart, she looked at the store newspaper to see what was on sale.

As Emmy turned the pages of the store newspaper, she saw a special sale on pie fillings. It read: BUY ONE, TAKE ONE HOME FREE.

"What a fabulous, fantastic sale!" Emmy cried. She grabbed her cart and ran to the baking products aisle.

Emmy found the cans of pie filling and read the labels—
cherry, blueberry, pumpkin, apple, gooseberry, plum,
apricot, strawberry, lemon custard, and pecan.

Then she counted them—one, two, three, four, five, six,
seven, eight, nine, ten.

"Ten different kinds of pie filling," Emmy said. "I'll
make one pie with each kind of filling and put all of them
in the freezer. Then I'll have ten ready-to-eat pies!"

Emmy piled her shopping cart full of pie filling cans.
She bought the other ingredients she needed, and headed
for home.

When Emmy arrived home, she rushed into her kitchen and started to bake. She baked and baked and baked and didn't stop until all ten of her pies were finished.

Emmy decided to let them cool on the porch. So she spread the store newspaper on the table and carefully set her ten pies out on top of it. Then she wrote the name of each kind of filling on a little tag and stuck them in the pies so she could tell which was which.

"Yum, yum, yum," she said out loud. "These pies look absolutely scrumptious. I'll taste one as soon as they are cool enough." Emmy wiped her hands and went back to the kitchen to clean up.

Soon, Vinnie the Vocal Vulture and Nelly the Naughty Newt came by and saw the ten pies on Emmy's porch. Then they saw the words on the store newspaper saying TAKE ONE HOME FREE.

"Well, well, well! How gracious of our kind friend, Emmy!" Vinnie exclaimed as he inspected the pies. "Ten beautiful pies—and we each get to take one. I don't care for gooseberry pie, but I do enjoy all of the others. So many choices! I can't decide which one I want."

While Vinnie was chattering away, Nelly made up her mind and ran off with the lemon custard pie.

"I took one pie," she called over her shoulder. "So now there are only nine for you to choose from."

Just as Nelly left, Katy the Kind Koala came walking by. She saw Vinnie looking at the pies and the words TAKE ONE HOME FREE.

"Goodness! How kind of Emmy to share her pies!" Katy said. "Which one are you taking, Vinnie?"

"I don't know," Vinnie answered. "Not the gooseberry, for sure."

"I see there are nine pies here," Katy said. "If I take one away, there will still be eight pies for you to choose from." Katy took the apple pie and waved a cheery goodbye.

"Well, now," Vinnie said. "Where was I? Ah, yes. Pies—eight pies. Which one should I choose?"

"What are you doing, Vinnie?" asked Lizzy the Lazy Lamb as she stopped to rest on Emmy's porch steps.

"As you can see, Lizzy, my dear," Vinnie said, "there are eight pies here. Emmy is graciously giving them to us. But I can't decide which one to take."

"Oh, goody," Lizzy said. "I'd love to take the strawberry pie. Then I won't have to bother making dessert." Lizzy took her pie and wandered off.

"Ahem! Now there are seven pies left, and one of them is the gooseberry, which I definitely don't care for," Vinnie said.

Just then, Ziggy the Zippy Zebra and Ivy the Impatient Iguana came jogging by.

"Hi, Vinnie," Ziggy called. "We heard Emmy has baked some pies for us. Are you in charge of giving them out?"

"Well . . . er . . . ah . . . ," Vinnie started to explain.

But Ivy interrupted. "I'm in a big hurry!" she said, looking at the seven pies. "If you don't mind, I'll just grab this cherry pie and be on my way."

"And I'll take this pumpkin pie," said Ziggy. "It's my favorite."

So Ziggy and Ivy picked up their pies, thanked Vinnie, and jogged off.

Vinnie turned back to the table to see how many pies were left.

"Let's see, there were seven pies, and Ivy took one, leaving six," he said. "Then Ziggy took one away, and now there are five pies left to choose from."

"Five pies," Vinnie muttered. "Five, five, five. Five pies are here and five have already been taken."

Not long after, Vinnie saw Bradley the Brave Bear riding by on his bicycle.

"Bradley, my friend," he called. "Emmy baked ten pies today, and, as you can see by this sign, she wants us each to take one home. Nelly, Katy, and Lizzy each took a pie, so then there were seven left. Just now, Ivy took the cherry pie, leaving six, and then Ziggy took the pumpkin pie, leaving five pies here to choose from. Will you help me pick a pie? I like them all, except the gooseberry."

Bradley looked at the five pies and said, "Sorry, I can't make up your mind for you, Vinnie, but I know which one I'd like." So Bradley took the pecan pie, wished Vinnie luck with his decision, and rode off.

"My, my!" Vinnie said. "Now there are only four pies."
He was still trying to decide which one to take when he
heard Herbie the Happy Hamster's cheerful voice.

"Hi, Vinnie! Isn't it a beautiful day!" Herbie called. "The
sky is blue, the sun is shining, and I understand we get to
have a free pie—thanks to Emmy."

Herbie looked over the four pies and took the blueberry
one. "Now there are three pies left," Herbie said. "Have a
good day, Vinnie."

As Vinnie stared at the three remaining pies, Una the Unhappy Unicorn arrived.

"Oh, dear," Una cried, looking at the pies. "I see a plum, an apricot, and a gooseberry. How I wish there were a rhubarb pie. I just love rhubarb pie, but I guess apricot will have to do."

Una dabbed her eyes with her hanky, took the apricot pie, and went on her way.

This left two pies on the table—and one of them was gooseberry.

TAKE ONE HOME FREE

"Now, as I was saying," Vinnie mumbled. "There are two pies—a plum and a gooseberry. I do believe I know which one I want now."

But just as Vinnie was about to reach for the plum pie, he felt someone tap him on the shoulder. It was Justin the Joking Jackal.

"Hello, Justin," Vinnie said. "You're just in time to get the last pie—the gooseberry."

But Justin didn't want the gooseberry, so he tried one of his favorite tricks.

"Vinnie! Look! Look at all those beautiful clouds!" he cried, pointing to the sky.

The minute Vinnie turned to look up, Justin grabbed the plum pie and ran off, laughing.

Vinnie stared at the one pie that remained on the table.

"Hmm," he said. "I see there's just one pie left—and it is the gooseberry. My mind is made up at last! Gooseberry, looseberry, mooseberry pie. Perhaps I'll like it if I try."
So Vinnie took the last pie and started to walk away. Just then, Emmy's back door opened.

"My pies must be cool by now," Emmy thought as she came out to the porch. "I can hardly wait to taste my very favorite of all—gooseberry pie."

But when she walked over to the table, Emmy couldn't believe her eyes.

"My pies! My pies!" she cried. "Where are my ten beautiful crunchy, munchy, crispy, crusty pies? They're all gone! There are no pies left!"

Vinnie heard the commotion and went back. Feeling a little confused and embarrassed, he tried to explain. "Well, my dearest Emmy," he began. "Nelly took one pie, and that left nine. Then Katy took one, leaving eight. Lizzy took one away, leaving seven. Ivy took one, and six remained. Then Ziggy took one, and five were left. Bradley took one, and then there were four. After Herbie took one, there were only three. When Una took one, there were two. Then Justin took one, leaving the last pie. And that's what I have here— the gooseberry."

Then Emmy noticed the store newspaper on her porch table with the words TAKE ONE HOME FREE. "Oh dear, dear me," she said. "Now I understand."

Emmy looked at the pie Vinnie was holding. "Well, at least the last pie is my all-time favorite—gooseberry," she added. "Would you share it with me, Vinnie?"

"Why, I'd be delighted, my dear Emmy," Vinnie said. He took Emmy's knife, cut the pie in two, and put half on her plate.

Then Vinnie said, "Now I have only half the pie, but I'll enjoy it twice as much because we'll be enjoying it together, my dear Emmy. And if I've said it once, I've said it a hundred . . . no, a thousand times . . . a shared pie is the very best pie of all!"

Look back at the pages of this book to find out which AlphaPet took each of the ten pies pictured on this page.

lemon custard

cherry

plum

apricot

pumpkin

gooseberry

apple

strawberry

pecan

blueberry

Know Your Alphabet

Aa Bb

Gg Hh

Mm Nn Oo Pp

Uu Vv Ww